A DAVID FICKLING BOOK

Text copyright © 2010 by Lee Weatherly
Jacket art and interior illustrations copyright © 2010 by Joanna Harrison

All rights reserved. Published in the United States by David Fickling Books, an imprint
of Random House Children's Books, a division of Random House, Inc., New York.
Originally published in Great Britain by David Fickling Books, an imprint of Random
House Children's Books, a division of the Random House Group Ltd., London, in 2010.

David Fickling Books and the colophon are trademarks of David Fickling.

Visit us on the Web! www.randomhouse.com/kids

Educators and librarians, for a variety of teaching tools,
visit us at www.randomhouse.com/teachers

Library of Congress Cataloging-in-Publication Data
Wells, Kitty.
Shadow magic / Kitty Wells ; [illustrations by Joanna Harrison]. — 1st American ed.
p.   cm. — (Pocket cats)
Summary: A small ceramic cat comes to life to help Maddy's cousin Chloe, who is
staying with her and is having trouble adjusting to a new school.
ISBN 978-0-385-75200-8 (trade) — ISBN 978-0-375-89801-3 (ebook)
[1. Cats—Fiction. 2. Magic—Fiction. 3. Moving, Household—Fiction. 4. Schools—
Fiction. 5. Cousins—Fiction.] I. Harrison, Joanna, ill. II. Title.
PZ7.W46485Sh 2011
[Fic]—dc22
2010029508

Printed in the United States of America
July 2011
10 9 8 7 6 5 4 3 2 1

First American Edition

Pocket
·Cats·

Shadow
Magic

Kitty Wells

illustrated by Joanna Harrison

David Fickling Books

OXFORD · NEW YORK

Also by Kitty Wells

Paw Power
Feline Charm

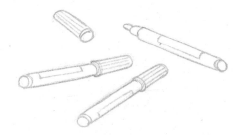

Chapter One

Maddy Lloyd put down her marker and gazed at the brightly coloured sign she'd just made. WELCOME CHLOE!!! it read, with flowers and rainbows dancing around the letters. *Perfect!* she decided. Standing on her bed, she stuck the sign to her bedroom wall with Blu-Tack.

"What do you think?" she asked the ceramic cats that sat on her desk.

There were three of them: a grey one,
a black and a tabby, all sitting together
with their tails and paws entwined.

Maddy waited hopefully for a
moment, but the tiny figures just
gazed silently back at her, their
painted eyes unblinking. With a sigh
of disappointment, she hopped down
off the bed.

Not long ago, Maddy wouldn't have

expected a response from the ceramic figurines . . . but something amazing had happened recently. The grey cat, who was called Greykin, had actually *come to life* – and had explained that one of the three cats would always do so whenever there was a problem that needed their attention.

A wonderfully magical time had followed as Maddy and Greykin solved the problem that had faced them. Next it would be the turn of one of the other cats. But when? Maddy wistfully touched their smooth heads, longing to feel the small, furry warmth as one of them came to life again.

Never mind, she told herself. *It'll happen sometime – Greykin promised. And meanwhile, Chloe's coming!*

Excited butterflies fluttered through Maddy's stomach. She didn't see her cousin very often, because the Taylors moved around so much. But now Chloe, Aunt Lily and Uncle Greg were actually moving to Maddy's town. Even better, they were all going to stay with the Lloyd family for a few weeks until they could move into their new house.

Maddy looked around happily. She could hardly wait for Chloe to see her room! A few months ago Maddy's father had painted it in her favourite colours, pink and yellow, and she was sure Chloe would love it as much as she did.

Shadow Magic

Suddenly a thought came to Maddy, and she frowned. Chloe would be sharing her room, and her cousin could be a bit careless at times. What if she accidentally knocked over the cats?

Maddy shivered, imagining it. Rummaging through her chest of drawers, she pulled out a red silk handkerchief that her grandmother had given her. Gently wrapping the cats in it, she put them in her desk drawer.

"There," she said aloud as she closed it. "Just to be on the safe side."

Glancing in the mirror, Maddy quickly pulled her long brown hair into a ponytail. It was still very strange to think that she was just ordinary Maddy Lloyd – smaller than most of the girls in her class, with an annoying sprinkling of freckles across her nose and a pair of very commonplace blue eyes – and yet she somehow had the most wonderful secret in the entire world!

Suddenly Maddy gasped as she heard a car pull into their drive. They were here!

She dashed out onto the landing, almost colliding with her little brother, Jack. The two of them thundered down the stairs just as their mother opened the front door.

"Lily!" Mum cried, embracing her younger sister. All at once it was chaos,

with what seemed like dozens of bags everywhere, and everyone crowding into the front hallway at the same time.

Dad shook Uncle Greg's hand. "Good to see you! Here, let me help you with that . . ." He took a suitcase from him.

Jack was hanging onto Uncle Greg's other arm. "Did you bring me any new Monster cards? Did you?"

"Maybe." Uncle Greg laughed and handed him a plastic-wrapped pack. With a whoop of excitement, Jack raced off into the lounge.

"And Maddy! How's my girl?" said Aunt Lily, scooping her into a hug.

"Hi, Aunt Lily." Returning the hug, Maddy craned round to see through the front door. Chloe was just coming up the path with a large purple

8

and silver handbag slung over one
shoulder. She was wearing a set of
earphones, and she looked bored.

Maddy blinked, taken aback. Wasn't
she happy to be here?

As Chloe reached the front door,
she pulled out one of her earplugs.
"Hi, Aunt Jenny. Hi, Uncle Ted."

Feeling oddly shy, Maddy hung back as her parents gave Chloe a hug. Her cousin had grown several inches since she'd last seen her, and looked very grown up.

Then Maddy told herself she was being silly. This was *Chloe* – the same cousin she used to have sleepovers with, sitting up half the night giggling together over daft jokes!

"Hi, cuz," she said eagerly.

Chloe smiled, but didn't really look at her. She was too busy twirling the dial on her iPod. "Hi," she said.

Maddy hesitated. Chloe's wavy blonde hair had been cut into a stylish bob, she noticed. All at once her long ponytail seemed very babyish.

But maybe it was just because they were with the rest of the family that

10

things felt so awkward. Once they were on their own together, her cousin would surely be her old self again.

"Chloe, come and see my room!" urged Maddy. "It looks really different now." But her cousin had taken out a mobile phone, and was busy typing a text with her thumb. Had she even heard?

"Yes, let's go up and get everyone settled," said Mum. "Then we can have a cup of tea. Lily, you and Greg must be gasping for one!"

As they all headed up the stairs, Maddy felt deflated. Chloe was trailing along behind them, still tapping out a text like she didn't even care. But she was sure to love the pink and yellow room – not to mention the welcome sign Maddy had made!

Mum smiled at her as they reached the landing. "Show everyone your room, sweetie."

"Yes, have a look at my handiwork!" said Dad to Aunt Lily and Uncle Greg. "I'll put these away for you." Taking their luggage, he staggered off towards the spare room.

Maddy hesitated, glancing back

at Chloe. She had hoped to get her cousin on her own, not with the adults there as well. Still, they'd have lots of time together, Maddy reassured herself. Chloe would be sharing her bedroom for weeks!

"Here it is," she said, swinging open the door.

"Oh, how pretty!" exclaimed Aunt Lily as she stepped inside. "I love the little flowers."

"Yes, aren't they sweet? Maddy made the stencils herself," said Mum.

"Chloe! Come and look at the sign," said Uncle Greg, drawing her into the room. Maddy held her breath expectantly as her cousin looked up at the brightly coloured welcome sign.

Chloe gave a forced smile. "Thanks," she muttered, not looking as if she was really pleased at all.

Maddy's own smile faded. It was as if she had done something wrong – but what? Aunt Lily put an arm around her. "It was very sweet of you to make a sign," she said, giving her daughter a hard look.

Chloe nodded unenthusiastically. "Yeah, it's great." She cleared her throat. "Um, Aunt Jenny . . . where am I going to sleep?"

Maddy stared at her. "You're sleeping in here with me!" she burst out.

Mum looked flustered. "Well – that *is* what we'd planned, Chloe. Maddy's got a double bed, and you two girls have always shared before . . ."

Chloe's jaw dropped. "But that was ages ago!" she protested. "I'm in secondary school now; I need

15

a lot more privacy."

"This isn't a hotel, Chloe," pointed out Uncle Greg with a frown. "You'll sleep wherever it's convenient for you to."

Maddy gazed at her cousin in hurt disbelief. Chloe didn't even look at her. "But I *can't* share with Maddy," she insisted. "Honestly, Aunt Jenny, I stay up so much later than she does now, doing homework and stuff – I'll fall behind if I have to go to bed when she does!"

Maddy's face grew hot. Chloe was acting like she was a million years older than she was, not just two and a half!

"Well . . ." Mum began helplessly.

Dad came into the room behind them. "What about my study?" he

16

suggested. "There's a sofa bed in there, and you can close it off from the lounge with those doors, just like a bedroom."

"Ted, are you sure?" asked Aunt Lily anxiously. "We don't want to put you out, but maybe—"

"Oh, yes please!" cried Chloe, her face alive with hope. "Please, Uncle Ted, please, please, please!"

Maddy's throat felt tight. She'd been looking forward to seeing Chloe for weeks, and now her cousin was acting like sharing with her would be the worst thing in the world!

"Well, let's pop down and see what you think," said Dad. "You don't mind, do you, Maddy?" He touched her head, looking as if he understood how she felt.

Maddy lifted a shoulder. "No, I don't care," she said stiffly. "Chloe can sleep wherever she wants."

As everyone left to go downstairs, Mum gave Maddy a quick hug. "Don't worry, darling," she whispered. "Chloe's getting to a funny age, that's all. Why don't you come down and have a cup of tea with us before dinner?"

Maddy shook her head. With a final

squeeze her mother left her alone,
shutting the door behind her.

Gazing sadly around her pink and
yellow room, Maddy realized that
Chloe hadn't said a single word about
how nice it looked. She was probably
too *grown up* to like pink any more!

Struggling to hold back tears,
Maddy jumped onto her bed and
yanked down the welcome sign. She
started to chuck it in the bin, and

then hesitated. The flowers and rainbows were really too pretty to throw away.

Grouchily she shoved the sign under her bed. She was *glad* Chloe wasn't going to be sharing with her. Her cousin wasn't nice at all any more – acting so snooty and grown up, with her mobile and her iPod!

Suddenly Maddy froze. What was that? She had heard something – a faint yowling, hissing noise, like . . .

Like a cat!

Lunging for her desk, Maddy slid open the drawer. The red silk handkerchief was bucking about as if it had a frog in it. She gaped at it in horror. One of the cats had come to life, and was now trapped! How could

21

she have been so daft?

"It's OK," she soothed, trying to tug the struggling parcel towards her. The spitting and snarling grew louder. The handkerchief wriggled out of her grasp.

"It's OK!" repeated Maddy frantically, raising her voice. "Just be still, and I'll get you out!"

The handkerchief was still again. Carefully Maddy picked it up. She could feel two ceramic cats inside, along with the tiny, warm weight of the one that had come to life.

But which one? Maddy's heart pounded as she put the handkerchief down on her desk and began to unwrap it. As the last fold of silk fell away, a small dark blur shot past Maddy's ear.

"Oh!" she cried, jerking back in surprise.

The black cat landed on the desk clock and spun to face Maddy. Her fur was dishevelled, and her bright green eyes flashed like jungle fire.

"There was *really* no need to imprison me like that!" she huffed indignantly.

Chapter Two

Maddy's hair felt electric as she looked at the little cat. The magic had happened again; it really had! The cat was only five centimetres tall . . . and *alive*. Her slim black tail twitched crossly as she regarded Maddy.

Suddenly Maddy realized that the cat was waiting for an answer. "I'm – I'm really sorry," she stammered. "I was worried that you might get knocked over, that's all."

"Well, better knocked over than *that*," retorted the cat, scowling at the handkerchief. Pointedly she began grooming herself, muscles rippling under her dark fur.

Maddy couldn't take her eyes off her. A neat, tidy little cat; and entirely black, like midnight with no stars. The only thing that wasn't inky was the startling green of her eyes.

"I'm really sorry," said Maddy
again. "But I'm so pleased to meet
you! What are you called?" She held
her breath eagerly.

The cat stopped washing herself and
stared at Maddy in silence. She was
much smaller than Greykin, with a
sleek feminine slenderness.

"I'm Nibs," she said finally.

Maddy longed to stroke the tiny
cat, but wasn't sure whether she'd
been forgiven yet. Besides, Nibs
didn't look terribly cuddly. In
fact, her unblinking gaze was a bit
disconcerting.

Remembering that the cats' magic
worked better if they were touching,
Maddy rearranged Greykin and the
tabby so that they were entwined once
more. She bit her lip, trying to think

27

of something else to say.

"What's that?" asked Nibs suddenly, nodding at something on the desk.

Maddy glanced down. "Oh! It's a calculator. It does sums." She turned it on and showed Nibs 7 + 3.

The cat watched intently. "Interesting."

Maddy put down the calculator, and Nibs jumped up onto it. Balancing on the plastic keyboard, she punched in a few numbers with her paws: *8374940*, read the screen.

"Right. So we've moved on from paper and pencil, then," observed Nibs, hopping off the keyboard.

"When was that?" asked Maddy, leaning forward. She and her best friend, Rachel, had never been able to pin Greykin down as to the cats' history, and she was dying to find out more about them. All she knew for sure was that she herself had bought them at an antique fair in London.

Nibs gave her a look. Settling down onto her haunches, she curled her tail about her legs, her fur so dark that it was difficult to tell which was which. The silence grew around them.

Maddy swallowed.

Greykin had been *so* easy to talk to,
but somehow Nibs, with her staring
green eyes, wasn't the same at all.

"Are you hungry?" she asked
finally. "I could go and get you a bit
of ham, or—"

"No, thanks," said Nibs. "I'll take
care of my food myself."

"Oh." Maddy felt a bit crestfallen.
Greykin had loved it when she'd
snuck titbits from the kitchen up to
her room for him. She found herself
chewing her finger. "Well . . . would
you like anything else?"

"Mm. I should like to have a bed
somewhere," admitted Nibs, gazing
around the bedroom.

Maddy's spirits soared. Of course!
"I've got the *perfect* bed," she said
with a grin. "You're going to love it,

30

I promise." She held out her hand, palm up, so that Nibs could climb onto it.

The little cat stared at her palm without moving. Maddy's cheeks grew warm, and she dropped her hand to her side. "Um . . . it's over here," she mumbled, moving across the room to her chest of drawers.

In a sudden streak of black, Nibs leaped from the desk to the chair, and from there to the floor. Maddy's eyes widened. It was a huge jump for such a little creature; Nibs was smaller than one of Jack's hamsters! But the cat seemed unperturbed as she padded across the carpet.

"Here," said Maddy, pointing to a long strip of cardboard that leaned against the side of her chest of

drawers. She and Rachel had made
it into a ladder for Greykin, with bits
of Blu-Tack for steps, and it had been
great fun to see him climbing up and
down it.

Nibs was up the ladder in a flash.
Prowling atop Maddy's chest of
drawers, she found the ballerina
jewellery box for herself. Maddy
had left it just the way it was when
Greykin had slept there, with his little
bed of hair-scrunchies tucked in one
pink satin corner.

Rising up onto her hind legs, Nibs
peered into the box, her black tail
lashing from side to side. She gazed at
the bed for a long moment, and then
dropped down again.

Maddy's heart sank. "Don't you like
it?"

"*Greykin* slept there," said Nibs, peering up at Maddy with her unblinking green eyes. "I should like a bed that's my own."

"Oh." Somehow Maddy felt that she had made a terrible blunder. She looked helplessly around her room, wondering where else the tiny cat could sleep. The answer came to her in a flash.

"Wait right there!" she said.

Hurrying over to her toy box, Maddy dug through layers of old dolls and discarded board games. Finally she got to the very bottom, where her plastic Barbie house lived. She hadn't played with it for ages – she really preferred cuddly toys to Barbie – but it was just Nibs's size!

She placed it proudly on the floor.

34

Shadow Magic

The little cat padded down the ladder
and was beside her in an instant,
sniffing at it.

"What do you think?" asked
Maddy.

Nibs didn't answer. She stepped
delicately into the house, gazing at its
pink walls.

"And look, it has furniture," added
Maddy, diving into the toy box again.
She found table, chairs and bed, and
put them in the house.

Nibs nosed the plastic bed. "Too
hard," she commented.

Maddy took a blue woollen sock
out of a drawer and arranged it into a
soft nest on the bed. Nibs leaped up
and tried it out, turning around several
times before finally curling up on the
sock like a sleek black comma.

Maddy held her breath.

"Yes, this will do," said Nibs, blinking up at her.

Maddy's heart sang as if she had just been given a hundred birthday presents all at once. "Great!" she said happily. She crouched down beside the doll's house. "Nibs, you're here because there's a problem, right? Do you have any idea what—"

Her bedroom door opened, and her mother peered in. "It's almost time for dinner, Maddy. Oh, you're playing with your doll's house! You haven't had that

out in ages." Mum leaned against the
doorframe, gazing at it fondly. She
had always liked dolls more than
Maddy did, even if *she* was the adult.

"I know, I just . . . felt like it," said
Maddy lamely, getting to her feet. She
wasn't in the least surprised to see
that Nibs had become ceramic again,
frozen on the miniature bed.

"Sweetheart, why don't you try
again with Chloe?" suggested Mum
as they went downstairs. "I'm sure
she didn't mean to hurt your feelings
before."

In all the excitement over Nibs,
Maddy had almost forgotten about her
cousin. She shrugged casually. "My
feelings aren't hurt," she said.

But of course they had been, and it
didn't help to see how settled Chloe

was in Dad's study. Her purple and silver bag was on his desk, and there was a folded duvet on the sofa. Chloe lay flopped on top of it, sending another text.

"Hi," said Maddy, standing in the doorway.

"Hi," said Chloe without glancing up.

Maddy shifted her feet. Part of her longed to tell Chloe about Nibs – she'd be impressed enough to look up from her mobile *then*. But Maddy knew she couldn't give the secret away to just anyone. Besides, this new, grown-up Chloe would never believe her.

"Mum says you're starting at your new school tomorrow," she said finally.

Chloe grimaced. "S'pose," she muttered.

"It's just across the street from our primary school," volunteered Maddy. "So, um . . . maybe I'll see you out on the playground or something."

Chloe looked up at that. "Maddy, we don't *play* in secondary school," she said pointedly. "So you probably won't see me, OK?"

Maddy felt her cheeks turn pink. *Good!* she wanted to shout. *Who wants to see you, anyway?* She bit back the words as Mum called them for dinner.

At least she had Nibs, Maddy told herself as they all sat down. A magical cat was better than a snooty cousin any day! Eager to get back to her room, she ate as quickly as she could, wolfing down her shepherd's pie.

"Easy, Miss Piggy!" said Dad. "You'll give yourself a conniption." The extra leaf had been put in the dining table, and the adults were all sitting down at the other end, drinking wine and laughing.

"Miss Piggy!" snorted Jack. "Oink, oink!"

Chloe let out a pained breath,

41

as though she couldn't bear being around either of them. Aunt Lily had made her take her earplugs out while she ate, but Maddy could tell she wished she still had them in, so that she wouldn't have to talk to anyone.

The moment Maddy had finished she laid her knife and fork across her plate. "Thank-you-for-dinner-may-I-please-leave-the-table?" she rattled off.

"No pudding?" said Mum in surprise.

"No, thank you."

Mum shrugged. "All right, go on then."

Chloe jumped up as well. "I'm finished too, Aunt Jenny. Uncle Ted, is it OK if I check my email on the computer in my room?"

Her room, thought Maddy heatedly as she ran up the stairs. Chloe had only had Dad's study for a few hours, and she was already taking it over! Well, she was welcome to it. Maddy had the most wonderful secret in the world in *her* room.

She shut her bedroom door behind her and dropped eagerly to her knees in front of the Barbie house. "Nibs, I'm back! I ate as fast as I could—"

Maddy broke off. The woollen sock bed was just as she had left it . . . but there was no sign of the tiny black cat.

She sprang to her feet. "Nibs!" she whispered, looking around. "Nibs, where are you?"

A frenzied search of her bedroom revealed nothing at all. Maddy looked under her bed, behind her desk, deep in her wardrobe . . . and found only dust balls and forgotten toys.

Shadow Magic

"Greykin, where has she gone?"
she asked the ceramic cat on her desk.
He and the tabby sat stiff and silent,
unable to reply: only one cat at a
time could come to life; the other two
had to remain ceramic, providing the
magical energy needed by the third.

Even so, Maddy thought Greykin
looked sympathetic. She stroked his
smooth grey head, close to tears. Had
she only imagined Nibs coming to

life? No, that was impossible! The black cat was missing from the trio, and then there was the sock bed as well.

She'll come back soon, Maddy told herself, trying to calm down. *She has to!*

But the little cat still hadn't reappeared by the time Maddy went to bed. After Mum had turned out her light, Maddy curled up under her flowered duvet, feeling very alone.

First her cousin didn't seem to want to know her – and now Nibs was gone too.

Chapter Three

Maddy's sleep was full of
unsettling dreams about finding
treasure and then losing it again.
When she woke up, still feeling
bleary-eyed, it was to a slight pressure
on her arm. Turning her head, she
held back a gasp.

The tiny black cat was sitting on her
elbow, calmly washing herself with
long strokes of her pink tongue.

Joy bounded through Maddy.

"You're back!" she cried.

Nibs paused long enough to look surprised. "Of course."

"But" – Maddy sat up carefully, holding her elbow out from her side – "where *were* you? I looked everywhere!"

Nibs gave her a bland look. "Outside."

"*Outside?*"

Shadow Magic

Nibs nodded towards Maddy's old-fashioned sash window. It stood open a crack; Mum believed in having fresh air. Maddy's jaw dropped. "But – but, Nibs, we're practically out in the country! There's foxes, and – and weasels, and – *other cats*!"

With a push against Maddy's elbow, Nibs leaped onto the bedside table, where she perched on top of the little box of worry dolls. "I can take care of myself," she said matter-of-factly. "I was getting my dinner, actually."

"Getting your . . ." Maddy trailed off, suddenly realizing what Nibs meant. She thought of asking what the little cat had eaten, and then decided she really didn't want to know.

"Nibs, I've got to go to school today," she said instead, keeping

49

her voice low. "Would you like to come with me, so you can see if the problem we have to solve is there?"

Excitement tingled through her at the thought. Greykin had often travelled to school in Maddy's pocket. In fact, introducing him to her best friend, Rachel, had been practically the best part of the whole adventure!

Nibs had started to wash again, first licking one black-padded paw and then swiping it across her inky ears. "No need," she said. "I already know where the problem is."

Maddy stared at the tiny cat, disappointment

battling with surprise. "You do?"

Nibs paused mid-stroke, and regarded Maddy with her bright green gaze. "Yes. It's here, in this house."

Maddy went to school in a daze, trying to take in all that had happened in such a short while. In the playground she grabbed Rachel and drew her to one side.

"Rache, it's happened again," she whispered.

Her best friend understood immediately. "Which one?" she cried,

her blue eyes widening behind her glasses. "Have you got it with you? Can I see?"

"The little black one – she's called Nibs. And no, I don't. She, um . . . didn't want to come." Maddy felt her cheeks catch fire. Nibs was so different from the cuddly Greykin!

"Come on, tell me everything," said Rachel, pulling Maddy under the slide. There was a cosy space beneath it where the two of them often spent their break times.

Maddy quickly filled her in as they sat side by side on the tarmac. "Maddy, you numpty," Rachel giggled when she heard about the handkerchief. But she became serious again when Maddy told her where the problem was that needed to be solved.

"In your house? You mean . . . it might be something to do with your family?"

Maddy nodded, worry knotting her stomach.

"Or I suppose it could even be *you*, couldn't it?" mused Rachel, tucking back a strand of long blonde hair. Maddy stared at her. The thought hadn't occurred to her, and it wasn't a pleasant one.

"Didn't Nibs say what the problem was?" asked Rachel. There was a thundering noise above them as a group of boys attacked the slide.

"No," admitted Maddy. "She said she was tired, and needed a nap." Unable to stop herself, she burst out, "Oh, Rachel, she's not at all what I expected! She's so – so . . ."

"Standoffish?" offered Rachel.

"Yes!" exclaimed Maddy. "Greykin and I were friends right from the start, but Nibs . . ." She fumbled for words. "I – well, I just don't think she likes me very much."

Rachel rubbed her arm. "Maddy, don't worry! A lot of cats are like that – you have to get to know them before they'll warm to you. My aunt's cat avoided me for *years* before he finally let me stroke him."

"But I don't want to wait years!" wailed Maddy. "I want Nibs to love me *now*."

"Well, you *did* trap her in a handkerchief," Rachel pointed out with a grin. "Give her a chance."

Maddy hugged her knees with a sigh. Though she knew Rachel was probably right, her heart still ached for the chunky, lovable Greykin.

Rachel gave her a friendly nudge. "Anyway, at least your cousin Chloe is there, right? How are you getting on with her?"

Maddy nodded quickly. "Great! She's just as much fun as I remembered." She *couldn't* admit that Chloe didn't seem to like her either. In fact, Chloe and the aloof Nibs had a lot in common!

Luckily the bell rang before Rachel could ask anything else. As everyone trooped towards the front doors, Maddy gazed across the street at the secondary school. Chloe was in there right now, probably making lots of grown-up-acting friends.

I don't care, Maddy told herself firmly. *I didn't want to be her friend any more anyway!*

Even so, she couldn't help letting out a sigh as she and Rachel took their seats in the 5A classroom. She *wouldn't* care so much about Chloe . . . if only Nibs seemed a little friendlier.

The moment Maddy got home that evening, she hurried up the stairs

towards her room. "Maddy!" her
mum called after her. "Aren't you
going to say hello to Aunt Lily and
Uncle Greg?"

"Hi, Aunt Lily, hi, Uncle Greg!" she
flung over her shoulder.

Shutting her bedroom door, Maddy
could feel her heart hammering.
Would Nibs have vanished again? But
the tiny cat sat waiting for her on the
chimney of the pink Barbie house, her

black tail twitching with impatience.

"Where were you?" she demanded.
She jumped onto the plastic roof with
a tiny *thump*. "I've been waiting."

"Sorry," said Maddy breathlessly.
"I had ballet class after school." She
dumped her school bag on her desk
and crouched down beside the doll's
house. "Nibs, what's the problem that
we need to solve? How do you know
it's here in the house?"

Nibs didn't reply; she was
obviously finding the steep plastic
roof difficult. Maddy hid a smile
as the little cat slid gradually
downwards, claws scrabbling. With a
growl, Nibs tried to leap back to the
chimney – and shot down the roof like
a furry black ball.

Suddenly Nibs was hanging off the

58

edge by her front claws, the rest of her
dangling over the carpet.

"Um . . . can I help?" offered
Maddy.

"I'm perfectly all right, thank you,"
said Nibs coolly. She whipped from
side to side, hind legs churning as she
tried to climb back onto the slippery
roof. "I don't know what this – this
substance – is, but it's not at all

what I'm— *Rrowww!*"

The last was a yodelled shriek as one of Nibs's front paws slipped. Maddy quickly cupped her hand under the cat, and Nibs dropped onto it, quivering. Maddy could feel her heartbeat racing against her fingers, as if she was holding a frightened bird.

She set Nibs gently down on the carpet. The tiny cat sat staring up at her for a long moment, her green eyes unblinking. "It was all under control, you know," she said.

"Yes, of course," said Maddy gravely.

"I wasn't going to fall. I was merely – er . . ." Nibs turned her head with something like a cough. "Anyway. Thank you," she muttered.

"You're welcome," said Maddy.

There was an awkward pause.

"Right. This problem that we need to solve," said Nibs finally. "I know it's in the house because my whiskers were tingling when I first came to life."

"They were?" said Maddy.

Nibs nodded. "The problem is something to do with that girl who was in here yesterday."

A chill swept over Maddy. "You

mean *Chloe*?" she gasped. "But
– what's wrong with her? Is she
OK?" Though Chloe was being very
irritating at the moment, the thought
of anything happening to her was
terrible.

"Well, that's what we need to find
out," said Nibs briskly, flicking her
whiskers. "Where is she?"

"In her room, I suppose – I mean,
my dad's study." Maddy swallowed.
"Would – would you like to ride in
my pocket, and we can go and see?"

Nibs gave Maddy's pocket a
distrustful look, and Maddy guiltily
remembered the handkerchief. "No,
thank you," she sniffed. "I'll ride on
your shoulder. If you wear your hair
down, it should cover me."

Despite her worry, a thrill of

excitement swept through Maddy.
She put out her hand again. Stepping
onto it, Nibs padded matter-of-factly
up Maddy's sleeve to her shoulder.
There she crouched down, balancing

herself with her claws.

Maddy stood up slowly, careful not
to tip her off. Nibs was so different
from the relaxed Greykin! Her small
body felt poised with muscle, ready
for anything.

Glancing in the mirror, Maddy

pulled out her scrunchie and draped
her long brown hair over her shoulder,
hiding Nibs from view. Then, trying
to appear casual, she stepped out into
the corridor and wandered downstairs.

Chloe was sitting at Dad's
computer, writing an email. She
whirled round in her chair when
Maddy came in. "Don't you know
how to knock?" she said crossly.
Hitting a button, she quickly got rid of

what had been on the screen.

Maddy shrugged, keenly aware of the tiny cat perched on her shoulder. "Sorry, I forgot," she said. To her surprise, she saw a fantasy novel lying on the sofa with a bookmark halfway through it. The two cousins had always loved stories about different worlds, though Maddy would have thought that Chloe was too *grown up* to enjoy them now!

"Um . . . how was school?" she asked.

"Great. Wonderful." Looking away, Chloe swiped her eyes and grabbed a textbook out of her school bag. "Look, Maddy, do you actually want anything? Because I've got homework to do."

Maddy stared at her in confusion.

What was wrong? For a moment it had almost seemed as if Chloe was going to cry. And then all at once it hit Maddy: her cousin was *homesick*!

"You . . . you miss Ragdale, don't you?" she asked.

Chloe glared at her. "No, why would I?" she snapped, flipping open her textbook. "I'm used to leaving places; we do it all the time."

Maddy bit her lip. Though she'd never thought about it before, she suddenly realized how awful it would be if one of her parents had a job that moved them around so much. She imagined leaving Rachel, and winced.

"Were you writing to one of your friends just now?" she ventured. "I guess you must really miss them—"

Chloe's face went an angry red.

66

"I'm *fine*, Maddy!" she burst out, slamming her book shut. "Now, will you get out? I told you before, I'm busy!"

Chapter Four

Maddy backed out of the study, her thoughts tumbling wildly. No matter what her cousin said, she was sure she was right about her missing her old home and friends. Was *that* why Chloe was acting like this?

Back in the bedroom, Nibs nodded when Maddy shared her suspicions. "Yes, she's definitely homesick . . . but that's only part of the problem."

Shadow Magic

Maddy was standing in front of
the mirror, looking at the little cat
on her shoulder. "Only part of it?"
she echoed in dismay. Wasn't being
homesick bad enough?

"That's right." Nibs's tail lashed
urgently from side to side. "Unless we
can prevent it, something dangerous
will happen as a result of Chloe's
homesickness. I just can't tell *what*
yet."

Something dangerous? Cold prickles raced across Maddy's skin. "But . . . how can we stop it from happening when we don't know what it is?"

Nibs sprang from Maddy's shoulder onto the chest of drawers, where she sat beside a bottle of perfume taller than she was. She looked deep in thought. "It's something Chloe's going to do," she said finally. "But that's all I can see. You'll have to use your magic power to find out more."

Her magic power! Maddy caught her breath. When Greykin had come to life, he'd given Maddy the ability to do amazing feline feats. Performing giant leaps and whisking up trees like a squirrel had been incredibly exciting, and Maddy had been dying

70

to know what magic the other two cats could give her.

"Nibs, what *is* my—" she started, and then broke off as a tingling sensation swept through her. At the same moment her arm and hand seemed to *fade*, until only the faintest of outlines was left.

Maddy stifled a shriek. She could see the chest of drawers through her arm!

"This is your power," said Nibs, sounding pleased with herself. She too had gone faint – a ghost cat sitting beside the perfume. "You can become *shadowy*, like a cat slipping through the night. Rather good, isn't it?"

Looking down, Maddy saw that the rest of her had faded as well. "Sh-shadowy?" she stammered. She turned her hand this way and that, staring in wonder. She could hardly see herself!

"It's only temporary, of course," said Nibs. "But quite effective, if I do say so myself."

Maddy's alarm lessened as excitement leaped through her. "It's like being *invisible*," she breathed. She waggled her foot faintly in the air.

"Most people won't even notice you," agreed Nibs. She wrapped her shadowy tail neatly about herself. "Those who do will think you're just a trick of the light . . . or a ghost. It does take practice, though, or else—"

"Oh!" Maddy gasped as she suddenly popped back into view.

The little cat looked unsurprised. "Or else *that* happens," she finished dryly. "We'll start training as soon as possible."

"Jack, would you like to play hide-and-seek?" asked Maddy the next afternoon after school. Her little brother looked up from his Nintendo in surprise. Maddy didn't usually like playing games with him, because he got so cross if he lost.

"OK!" he agreed, scrambling up from the lounge floor.

Mum and Aunt Lily were sitting at the dining table having a cup of tea. For a change, Mum didn't say a word about homework. Instead she suggested, "Why don't you see if Chloe wants to play too?"

Maddy hesitated. Before she could make up an excuse, Chloe called out from the study, "No, I don't!"

Mum and Aunt Lily exchanged a

74

look, and Maddy realized that they
were worried about Chloe too. She
wished she could tell them she
was going to try and help her cousin,
but she knew that she could never
explain it!

"I get to hide first!" announced Jack
as they went outside.

"OK," agreed Maddy.

He dashed off as she shut her eyes

and began to count. When she got to
fifty, she glanced around and spotted
him easily, crouched down between a
tree and their fence.

Jack looked grumpy when she
tagged him. "There aren't enough
places to hide," he complained,
crawling out of the narrow space.
Then he brightened. "But that means
I'll find *you* really quickly too!"

"Go on, then," said Maddy, her
heart thumping.

Nibs had grudgingly agreed to ride
in her jacket pocket, and now Maddy
touched the ceramic cat nervously,
hoping she could remember all that
she'd been told. It would be awful if
she popped back into view right in
front of her brother!

Jack screwed his eyes shut and

leaned against the tree.
"One . . . two . . . three . . ."

There was a warm
shimmer as the little cat
came to life in Maddy's
pocket. Nibs bounded up
to her shoulder. "Are you
ready?" she whispered.

Maddy nodded, and the
tingling feeling rushed
through her like electricity. She stared
in fascination as she faded away to
barely a shadow. She could see the
grass through her feet!

Nibs tapped her ear with a stern
paw and Maddy caught herself,
remembering to concentrate. The cat
magic could turn her shadowy on its
own, but it needed her help to keep
her that way.

Shadow magic, conceal me, thought Maddy as hard as she could. The tingling grew stronger. *Shadow magic, conceal me . . .*

"Forty-eight, forty-nine, *fifty*!" Jack opened his eyes. "Ha! I see you!" he said.

Maddy froze. Had she reappeared already? But Jack ran straight past her towards the shed. Ducking behind it, he crowed, "That was way too easy, Maddy . . . Maddy?"

He came out again, frowning. She stood unseen in the middle of the garden as he poked about, looking behind each of the trees and even under the garden furniture.

"Where *are* you?" he muttered.

He looked so puzzled that Maddy had to hold her hands over her mouth

to stop herself laughing. She watched as he went down to the gate and stared into the meadow. Scratching his head, he even peered up at the trees. Maddy burst into giggles.

"Careful with the sniggering," cautioned Nibs. "You're about to—"

Whoosh! There was an almost audible popping sound as Maddy suddenly appeared again. She let out a disappointed breath. Her thoughts had been wandering, just like Nibs had warned her!

Jack turned back towards the house and saw her. His eyes bulged. "Where were you hiding?" he demanded, galloping up to her.

Maddy shrugged innocently. "Right here," she said.

"You were not!" cried Jack. "I

looked *everywhere!*"

"Not here, though," said Maddy, holding back a smirk.

Jack looked like a volcano about to erupt. "But there's no place to *hide* there!" he bellowed.

"Try another game," whispered Nibs, safely hidden behind Maddy's hair. "He looks as if he's enjoying it, really."

"Anyway, you didn't find me, so it's

my turn again," said Maddy. "Come on, Jack."

He glowered at her. "Fine! And this time I'm going to find you no matter *where* you hide."

During the next game Maddy concentrated hard, following Jack around the garden as he searched. Though almost ten minutes went by, she didn't flicker into sight once.

"Not bad," murmured Nibs in her ear. "Now practise coming into view again. Just think, *Shadow magic, leave me!*"

"Maddy, this isn't fair!" Jack was shouting. He stamped his foot. "You've gone back inside or something, haven't you?"

Grinning to herself, Maddy

82

crouched down behind a garden chair.
Shadow magic, leave me, she thought.
Shadow magic, leave me!

Tingling, she watched herself
slowly turn solid again, like a photo
coming into focus. Nibs leaped back
into her pocket just as the change
became complete.

"Here I am, Jack," called Maddy,
standing up and waving.

Her little brother spun round. "Where *were* you?" he gasped.

"Right there." Maddy pointed behind the chair.

"You were *not!*" shrieked Jack. "I looked there about a million times!"

Maddy shrugged. "I just kept moving around the chair so you wouldn't see me."

Jack stared first at Maddy and then at the chair, gaping in confusion.

"Good game!" she added brightly, barely managing not to laugh. "Do you want to play again?"

"No, I don't!" With a thunderous scowl, Jack shoved past Maddy into the house. "I'm going to go and play with my Nintendo. And *you* can't have a go!"

★

Shadow Magic

Back in Maddy's room, she and Nibs
began to plan. Now that Maddy could
use her shadowy skills, they decided
that she should sneak downstairs
that very night, while Chloe was still
awake. Using her powers, she could
slip unseen into Dad's study and see
if she could discover what her cousin
was going to do.

"How will I find out, though?"
asked Maddy doubtfully.

Nibs yawned, showing a pink mouth
and tiny white teeth. "How should I
know? Just have a look around. Maybe
you'll see something – a letter, or—"

"An email!" gasped Maddy. Of
course – her cousin had been writing
one just yesterday! Maybe she had
said something in it that would help
them.

"Email?" repeated Nibs blankly.
She was sitting inside the pink Barbie
house, her black fur gleaming like
satin.

Maddy explained that emails
were electronic letters. The little cat
twitched her ears. "Strange . . . Well,
couldn't you get a look at that?"

"I could try," said Maddy. Then
she frowned as an uncomfortable
idea came into her mind. "Um, Nibs
. . . isn't this sort of like spying on
Chloe?"

Nibs's green eyes widened in
surprise. "Yes, of course," she said.

"But – but that's wrong!" protested
Maddy.

Nibs stared at her. "How so?"

"Because whatever she's writing is
private!" said Maddy, exasperated.

86

"She wouldn't want me to see it."

Nibs looked unimpressed. "All right. Well, what do you suggest instead?"

Maddy screwed up her forehead as she thought. "Maybe I could just talk to her," she ventured. "I could ask her what's bothering her, and . . ."

"You tried that yesterday," pointed out Nibs.

Maddy fell silent as she realized

Nibs was right. She had tried to talk to Chloe, and it hadn't worked at all. Her cousin had just shouted at her.

Maddy nibbled the side of her thumb. "Is the problem very serious?" she asked in a small voice.

Though Nibs's expression didn't change, Maddy had the distinct feeling that the little cat wanted to roll her eyes! "I wouldn't be here if it wasn't," she said.

"All right," said Maddy reluctantly. "I'll do it."

"Good," said Nibs. Her muscles rippled under her dark fur as she pulled herself into a stretch. "Hopefully you'll find out what's going on, and then we can get this sorted. The sooner the better!"

Maddy bit her lip. She wanted to

help Chloe quickly too, but it still hurt
that Nibs didn't seem to care about
staying longer with her. Didn't she
like Maddy at all? Looking down,
Maddy played with a loose thread in
the carpet.

Greykin would have asked her what
was wrong, but Nibs didn't even

notice. She just hopped up onto the
Barbie bed, snuggling into Maddy's
sock. A moment later her eyes were
closed, her tiny sides rising and
falling.

Feeling discouraged, Maddy got
to her feet and left the sleeping Nibs

alone. Rachel had said that she just
had to be patient and give Nibs time
to warm to her . . . but how much
longer would she have to wait?

Chapter Five

"Goodnight, darling," said Mum, kissing Maddy's forehead. "Sweet dreams."

Maddy waited until her mother's footsteps had headed back downstairs, and then she sat up and switched on her bedside light.

"Ready?" said Nibs, leaping up onto the roof of the doll's house. Maddy had stuck tiny wedges of Blu-Tack onto it so that the little cat could get a

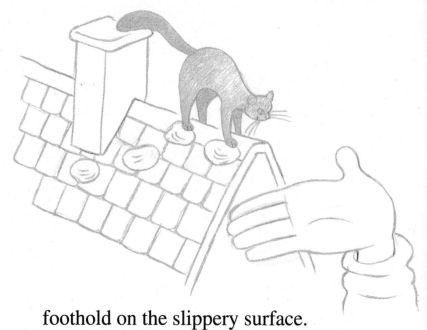

foothold on the slippery surface.

"Ready," whispered Maddy.

Crossing softly to the doll's house, she held out her hand. Nibs jumped onto it and padded up to her shoulder. "*Shadow magic, conceal me*," murmured Maddy as the tingling sensation washed over her. "*Shadow magic, conceal me . . .*"

Easing open her bedroom door,

she stepped invisibly out into the corridor. She could hear Jack snoring, and the adults talking and laughing downstairs. Chloe was probably in Dad's study, as usual . . . but Maddy would have to make it past both their parents to get there.

She went cold at the thought. What if her concentration broke like before, and she suddenly turned visible right in front of Mum and Dad? It would be too horrible for words!

"What are you waiting for?" hissed Nibs, nudging her ear with a tiny paw.

"Nothing," muttered Maddy. Greykin

would have understood her nerves,
but with the no-nonsense Nibs it
was a different matter. Squaring
her shoulders, Maddy stole down
the stairs and edged quietly into the
lounge.

"Gin," said Uncle Greg, spreading
a hand of cards onto the coffee table.
The other adults groaned good-
naturedly.

Maddy tiptoed past, focusing on the
magic as hard as she could. Just a few
more steps . . . almost there . . .

"What's that?" asked Mum
suddenly.

Maddy stifled a startled squeak.

"What's what?" said Dad.

Mum glanced around with a frown.
"I don't know – I thought I heard
something . . ."

Maddy gulped as her mother's gaze went right over her. *Shadow magic, conceal me!* she thought frantically. Peering down, she saw with relief that she was still shadowy – though she had never felt so visible in her life!

"Come on, Jenny, you're just trying to get out of another game," laughed Aunt Lily.

Finally Mum shrugged. "I must be imagining things," she said. "OK, deal me in!"

As the adults started playing again, Maddy hastily crossed the last few metres to the study. That was close! And she still had to sneak through the lounge a second time before she could return to bed. The thought made her mouth go dry.

But first she had to find out what the

96

problem was with Chloe.

The study door was open a crack.
Trying to make herself as thin as
possible, Maddy slipped through it.
Chloe was sitting at Dad's computer,
typing another email. The door
squeaked, and she quickly glanced up.

Maddy stood frozen, not daring to
move as her cousin suddenly got up
and started towards her. Had Chloe
seen her? No, it was impossible – she
was still invisible!

Chapter Five

Walking right past Maddy, Chloe shut the study door with a sharp *click*. "Stupid thing," she muttered. Returning to the computer, she sat down and began typing again.

Maddy gaped at the door. How was she supposed to get out now?

"Um . . . right," murmured Nibs in her ear. "We'll think about that later. Is that glowing thing an email?"

She meant the computer, Maddy realized. Pushing her worry aside, she crept forward. Chloe was perched cross-legged on Dad's chair, looking intently at the screen. Small black words appeared in the email box as she typed.

Stopping a few paces away, Maddy strained to read them. *Hi . . . Christy*? No, *Chrissy. It was sooo great to get*

*your email! This is much better than
texting, cos we've got lots to plan.
OK, how about next Saturday? I'll
get the train from here, and—*

A cold chill swept Maddy as she
read. The *train*? Where was Chloe
going?

All at once she heard footsteps
coming towards the study, and panic
crashed through her. She ducked for
cover behind an armchair. "Excuse

me?" whispered Nibs, lashing her tiny tail. "We're *invisible*, remember?"

Maddy's face grew warm. If she were visible, her cheeks would be blazing! She was just starting to get up when Aunt Lily came in. "Almost time for bed, Chlo— *Oh!*" she cried out as her foot hit Maddy's invisible leg.

"Ouch!" Maddy squawked, and then popped her hand over her mouth. It was too late. Not only had Aunt Lily heard her, but Maddy's concentration had shattered. The invisibility was gone.

Aunt Lily peered over the back of the chair. "Maddy? What are *you* doing in here?"

"Um . . . hi, Aunt Lily," she said. On her shoulder Nibs had become

ceramic again, and she quickly caught
the little cat before she tumbled down
the front of her nightie.

"*Maddy?*" Chloe burst out. A
moment later her cousin's furious face
joined her aunt's. "You were spying
on me!"

"No, I wasn't," protested Maddy
as she climbed to her feet. "I – I just
came in to say goodnight."

Glancing at the computer, she saw that her cousin had got rid of the email she'd been writing. Maddy's thoughts raced. Should she mention what she'd seen? But what if it was something totally innocent, and she got in trouble for snooping?

"We already *said* goodnight," Chloe pointed out, folding her arms over her chest.

"I know, but I wanted to, um . . . . show you my ceramic cat," said Maddy feebly, holding Nibs up.

Chloe gaped at her as if she were mad. "You've got to be joking!" she scoffed. "As if I'd even *care* about your stupid toy."

"Chloe . . ." said Aunt Lily
warningly.

Maddy glared at her cousin. Maybe
Chloe was upset about moving again,
but that didn't give her the right to
sneer at people! "Nibs is *not* a toy,"
she snapped, clutching the tiny cat to
her chest. "And I bet she's
a whole lot cleverer than
you are!"

Before Chloe could
reply, Mum appeared
in the study doorway.
"What's going on in
here?" She spotted
Maddy, and her face grew stern.
"I thought you were in bed, young
lady."

Maddy gulped. "I was . . . I just . . ."

Mum kept staring at her, her expression slowly turning to confusion. "Hang on – how did you get through the lounge without us seeing you?"

"She *sneaked*," put in Chloe angrily. "Just like she *sneaked* in here!"

"That's enough, Chloe!" said Aunt Lily, steering her daughter away from the desk. "Now come on, it's time to get ready for bed." The two of them left the study.

In the sudden silence, Mum opened her mouth and then closed it again. She rubbed her forehead. "Well, gosh, I must be going blind not to have seen you. Or else you're just very good at sneaking!"

"I guess I'm just very good at sneaking," agreed Maddy, red-cheeked.

Shadow Magic

"Back to bed now," said Mum. She held the door open for Maddy. "Come on, hip-hop."

Maddy slowly climbed the stairs behind Mum. Who was Chrissy, and where was Chloe planning on taking a train to? she wondered. Was she going on a day trip somewhere, maybe?

But she had no chance to talk to Nibs about it. Back in her bedroom, Mum put the ceramic cat on her desk and then tucked Maddy into bed.

"No more sneaking," she said firmly, kissing Maddy's cheek. Maddy nodded.

After Mum turned off the light, Maddy kept her gaze fixed on the ceramic figures, willing Nibs to come to life again. But the tiny feline remained statue-still, and finally Maddy's eyes closed despite herself.

Much later, there was a firm tap on Maddy's ear. A pause, and then there was another one. "Hey. Are you asleep?" demanded a voice.

"Mmph?" Groggily Maddy struggled to lift an eyelid – and then both eyes flew open. Nibs was sitting on the pillow beside her, her black fur gleaming in the moonlight.

"Nibs!" exclaimed Maddy softly.

106

She propped herself up on one elbow.
Coiling her tail around her legs, the
little cat cleared her throat. "Oh good,
you're awake. I just wanted to say . . .
thank you. For sticking up for me to
your cousin."

"That's OK," said Maddy, startled.
"I wanted to!" She grinned suddenly.
"I just wish Chloe could *really* see
you; then she'd see how wrong she

was. Her eyes would pop right out of her head!"

Nibs smirked. "Yes, we do have that effect on people." Her eyes glinted with wicked amusement.

The shared moment sent a warm feeling through Maddy . . . and then she remembered what had happened. She quickly sat up, crossing her legs and pulling the duvet around her.

"Nibs, what are we going to do?" she whispered. "I didn't get to read the whole email, and now—"

"I read it," broke in Nibs.

Maddy blinked. "You . . . did?"

Nibs nodded, her tiny face suddenly grave. "And the problem's just as bad as I feared. Your cousin's planning to run away."

Chapter Six

Maddy's blood turned to ice as she stared at the little cat. "Run *away*?" she squeaked. "You mean, back to Ragdale?"

Nibs flicked her ears in assent. "Yes, next Saturday. The plan is for Chloe's friend Chrissy to hide her somewhere in her house. But first Chloe has to *get* to Ragdale, and to do that she plans to take the train, and then a bus – and then she's going to hitchhike the last few miles."

"But she can't!" Maddy cried.
Popping her hand over her mouth,
she glanced at her bedroom door.
"Nibs, honestly, that's really, really
dangerous," she hissed. "She could be
kidnapped or something!"

"Yes, *dangerous* is certainly the
right word," agreed Nibs, flexing her
claws against the pillow. "We have to
stop her."

"Shall I tell my parents?" asked Maddy anxiously.

Nibs's green eyes looked doubtful. "You can try, but they probably won't believe you."

"But all they'd have to do is read Chloe's email!" cried Maddy. "Then they'd *have* to believe me."

Nibs started to prowl about. Her tiny weight barely made a dent in the pillow. "Except that the email isn't there any more. Chloe said that she was going to delete it after she sent it, and she asked Chrissy to do the same. I assume *delete* means to get rid of."

"Um . . . yes, it does," muttered Maddy in dismay.

Nibs paused in a gleam of moonlight. "Besides," she said matter-of-factly, "the magic wouldn't have

brought me to life if the problem
could be solved without your help."

Maddy shivered and drew the
duvet more tightly around her. "You
mean . . . I have to be the one to solve
it?"

Nibs nodded. "Yes. Well, both of us,
working together. If it could be solved
as easily as telling your parents, then
I wouldn't be here. That's the way it
works."

Maddy swallowed. Suddenly
having the magical cats seemed much
more serious than before. What if
she wasn't able to stop Chloe, and
something happened? Tomorrow
was Wednesday – they had just over
a week before she was going to run
away!

Amazingly, Nibs seemed to

112

understand how she felt this time.
"Worrying won't help anything, you
know," she said gently. Settling down
closer to Maddy, she curled herself up
on the pillow, no larger than a mouse.
"We can do it. I'm sure of it."

The next afternoon after school,
Rachel came home with Maddy to
help think of a plan. The moment they
got upstairs, she clutched Maddy's
arm eagerly. "Can I meet Nibs now?"
she begged. "I've been dying to!"

Bending down in front of the

Barbie house, Maddy motioned for
Rachel to join her. Nibs was lying
stretched out on the pink bed like a
tiny panther. She saw them and sat up,
gazing narrowly at Rachel.

"Who's this?" she demanded. Rachel sank to the floor, staring at Nibs in wonder.

"This is my best friend, Rachel," explained Maddy. "She's going to help us."

"Hello!" said Rachel, leaning forward. "I'm *very* pleased to meet you, Nibs. Would – would you mind if I stroked you?" She started to reach out with her hand and then stopped, confronted by Nibs's silent stare.

Rachel's cheeks coloured. "Or not," she mumbled, dropping her hand. "Um – sorry."

Though she knew it wasn't very nice of her, Maddy couldn't help feeling a bit glad. At least she wasn't the only one to get the silent treatment at times!

With a final hard look at Rachel, Nibs came out of the doll's house and padded across the carpet to Maddy. "Have you had any ideas yet?" she asked.

Maddy sighed, propping her chin in her hands. "No. Rachel and I tried to think of something at school today, but we couldn't come up with anything."

"We will, though," promised Rachel. She was still gazing at the tiny cat in awe, her blue eyes wide behind her glasses.

There was a pause as they all mulled over the problem. Suddenly Maddy started in surprise. As casually as if she did it every day, Nibs had settled down against Maddy's foot. Her tiny body was soft and warm, her black 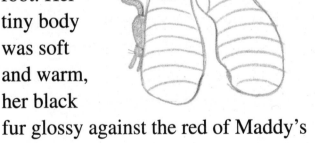 fur glossy against the red of Maddy's sock.

A glow of pleasure spread through

117

Maddy. Though she longed to stroke the little cat, she just sat very still. For now, it was enough that Nibs was snuggled up next to her!

Rachel was rubbing her glasses up and down her nose, which she always did when she was thinking hard. "We could lock Chloe in her room on Saturday," she suggested. "Or we could steal her shoes! Or . . ." She trailed off as Nibs stared wordlessly at her.

"You're not thinking big enough," stated the cat. "We need to stop Chloe from running away next Saturday, but there's more to it than that. The only way the problem can really be solved is if she's happy here. Otherwise she'll just try again. I know *I* would."

Maddy and Rachel exchanged a

doubtful glance. How could they make Chloe be happy when she wasn't? It sounded impossible!

Nibs raised an eyebrow as if she knew what they were thinking. "For instance, I wonder what it's like to start a new school?" she mused, scratching her ear. "I can't imagine it's very nice, really."

Rachel gasped. "Oh, Maddy, that's it!" she cried. "Just use your power to go into Chloe's school and get everyone to be friends with her, and then she'll change her mind about running away!"

Maddy's jaw dropped. "How am I

supposed to do *that*?" she protested.

Rachel waved her hand impatiently. "Lots of ways! You could – you could whisper in people's ears that Chloe Taylor is really nice, or you could make it so that people have to sit next to her in class, or all sorts!"

Maddy blinked as she realized that Rachel was right: there *were* a lot of things that she could do invisibly. In fact, it might even be fun!

"OK, I'll do it!" she said. "But I'd better practise being invisible a lot more first," she added with a sudden frown. The thought of suddenly appearing in the middle of Chloe's secondary school wasn't very appealing!

Nibs nodded. "We'll spend the weekend practising. Then you can go

120

into Chloe's school some day next week."

"Brilliant!" Rachel grinned, straightening her glasses. "I'm sure the plan will work. Just wait – Chloe will have millions of friends in no time!"

"Well, *millions* might be difficult to keep track of," said Nibs with a yawn. "Sometimes one friend is all you need. It's a good plan, though. Wish I'd thought of it." Curling herself into a cosy black circle, she started to close her eyes.

"Wait, Nibs . . . can I ask you something?" said Rachel, edging closer.

Nibs opened a single green eye and waited. Maddy smiled to herself, knowing what was coming.

Shadow Magic

Rachel took a deep breath, and said in a rush: "You see, Greykin never said much about where the three of you are from, and I just wondered if you could tell me more about it. You know, how old you are, and – and how the three of you came into being, and why . . ."

Nibs had both eyes open now, and was staring coldly at her. Maddy saw Rachel swallow..

"I mean . . . well, you don't *have* to tell me, if you don't want to," she stammered. "It's just that I'm going to be a scientist someday, so I'm sort of curious about these things, and . . . um . . ." Rachel's voice grew more and more feeble. Nibs hadn't blinked once as she gazed at her.

There was a pause.

"Never mind," said Rachel faintly. "I suppose I don't really need to know."

Nibs closed her eyes again, and went to sleep.

Just then the doorbell rang: Rachel's mother had arrived to take her home. Rachel looked a bit stunned as Maddy walked her downstairs. "She's very different from Greykin, isn't she?" she whispered.

Maddy nodded thoughtfully. "Yes, totally." And recalling the unexpected warmth of Nibs pressed against her foot, for the first time Maddy wasn't sure whether that was such a bad thing.

Then she sighed, remembering. If only the little cat wasn't so anxious to leave her!

That weekend Maddy went invisible every chance she could get. She slipped around the house like a ghost, unseen by her family. The magic felt much more serious now that she

knew she'd soon be sneaking into
Chloe's school, and she practised and
practised, until finally she got so good
at staying invisible that she thought
nothing at all could make her reappear
unexpectedly.

"Good," said Nibs briefly on
Sunday evening. She sat on the doll's
house chimney, her tail tucked neatly
around her legs. "I think we're ready."

Shadow Magic

On Monday morning Maddy waited until the kitchen was clear, and then darted in. Flipping quickly through the little phonebook that Mum kept by the telephone, she dialled her school's number. Nibs perched on the worktop, watching her closely.

"Good morning, Emerson Primary School," said Mrs Wooton's voice.

It was part of their plan that Maddy should call in sick that day, so that her teachers wouldn't suspect anything when she didn't go in. Mum, of course, would think that Maddy had gone to school as usual – but really, she'd be at the secondary school across the road, trying to make friends for Chloe.

Glancing around to make sure no one was nearby, Maddy held the

phone out to Nibs. The little cat purred into it, "Hello, this is Mrs Lloyd. Maddy's got a cold, so I'm keeping her home today."

Mrs Wooton chuckled. "You sound like you've got a frog in your throat yourself, Mrs Lloyd! All right then, we'll hope to see Maddy tomorrow."

Nibs looked insulted as Maddy hung up the phone. "A *frog*?" she echoed in disgust.

"It's just an expression," Maddy told her. "But, Nibs, we did it!"

Nibs smiled smugly as she leaped onto her arm. "Of course," she said, and settled herself on Maddy's shoulder.

"Bye, darling, have a good day," said Mum as she dropped Maddy off at school that morning.

"Bye, Mum," said Maddy, climbing out of the car. She tried not to look at the secondary school, in case she somehow gave herself away. Chloe was already there; Mum had dropped her off first.

As Mum drove away, Rachel hurried up to Maddy. "Are you ready?" she whispered excitedly. She pulled Maddy to one side of the playground, so that the two girls were hidden from view behind a tree.

Maddy nodded, touching the ceramic Nibs in her pocket. "I – I *think* so," she said. "But, Rachel, what if I can't find her or something?" She shivered at the thought. Now that it

was time to actually try their plan, she could imagine a hundred things that might go wrong!

Rachel adjusted her glasses. "Don't worry," she said. "I'm sure that—"

She broke off abruptly, gaping at Maddy. At the same time Maddy felt Nibs come to life, as well as the tingling sensation racing through her. She was going shadowy!

"*Wow*," breathed Rachel. Her eyes

were bulging. "Maddy, I can hardly see you! You're like a ghost or something!"

Nibs climbed out of Maddy's pocket and bounded up to her shoulder. "Right, then, are we ready to go and make friends?" she asked, swishing her tail from side to side. Maddy yearned to stroke her, but still didn't quite dare.

She took a deep breath. "Ready!" she said.

Chapter Seven

The secondary school was even larger than Maddy had imagined. The students were large too: most of them were about twice her size! *Shadow magic, conceal me*, Maddy thought fervently as she approached the main entrance.

A girl bumped into her. "Oh, sorry—" she started, and then broke off in confusion, looking around. "Weird . . ." she muttered, hurrying away.

To Maddy's relief, once she got inside she spotted Chloe almost immediately. Her cousin was leaning against a wall with her earphones on, looking down at her mobile.

Nearby, three girls around Chloe's age were peering around on the floor as if they'd lost something. Edging closer, Maddy suddenly realized that

she'd seen the girl with the long
chestnut ponytail before – her family
lived on the other side of the meadow
from the Lloyds.

Maddy's heart leaped. She had
always thought that the older girl
seemed really nice. She'd be a perfect
friend for Chloe, if only she could get
the two of them talking!

"But I had it just a minute ago!"
the girl was saying,
pulling fretfully at
her left earlobe.

"Can't either of
you see it?" In her
other ear twinkled
a tiny unicorn
earring.

One of her friends,
a tall blonde girl,

shook her head. "No, I can't see it anywhere, Gemma."

"I reckon you must have dropped it in your mum's car," said the third girl, who had short curly dark hair.

Gemma looked close to tears. "No, I definitely had them both on when I came into school!" she insisted, dropping to her knees to search. "Come on, you two, help me look."

A lost earring! Maddy's eyes widened. Could she and Nibs somehow use this to get the two girls talking?

Thinking hard, Maddy's gaze fell on the reception desk a couple of metres away. There was a gap under the desk, and she caught her breath as an idea came to her. "Nibs, I think I know where it might be!" she whispered.

Slipping invisibly past Gemma and

her friends, she crouched down and peered under the desk. It was so dark that at first she could hardly see a thing – but then, squinting hard, she suddenly saw something glinting on the floor.

"That's it!" purred Nibs. Leaping to the ground, the little cat padded off into the shadows, and a moment later returned triumphantly with the earring dangling from her mouth.

"Hurrah!" Maddy exclaimed

softly as Nibs leaped back onto her shoulder.

Taking the earring, she edged towards her cousin. Chloe was still gazing down at her mobile, punching keys with her thumb. Dropping the earring between Chloe's feet, Maddy quickly leaned over and touched her on the ankle.

"Huh?" Chloe started, and looked down. Seeing only the unicorn earring, she glanced around and spotted Gemma and her friends, still searching.

Chloe picked up the earring. "Hey, um – is this yours?" she asked, tapping Gemma's arm.

Gemma spun round. "My earring!" she cried, her face lighting up. "Oh, thank you, thank you! They were a

birthday present from my parents, and
I thought I'd lost one of them!" She
put it back in her ear, smiling broadly.

Chloe shrugged, looking embarrassed. "It was just on the floor over there—" She broke off as her mobile beeped with a text. "Oh – sorry," she said, and turned away to read it. Her eyes shining, Gemma went back to talking with her friends, the moment already forgotten.

The bell went then, and everyone started heading towards their classes. Trailing along after her cousin, Maddy clenched her fists in frustration. She had been so close to getting Chloe and Gemma talking – and then Chloe had to get another text and ruin everything!

"Never mind," murmured Nibs from her shoulder. "Try, try again, and all that."

✴

But by lunch time Maddy was feeling deeply discouraged. It wasn't nearly as easy to make friends for Chloe as she'd hoped. So far, she hadn't had even a single opportunity. Her spirits had lifted when Chloe's English class went to the library, but even there she hadn't had any chances. Chloe had immediately gone to the other end of the room from the others, and had spent the whole time just sitting on her own, reading her fantasy novel.

Maddy trailed glumly along behind as her cousin queued in the canteen. What was she going to do? Suddenly she caught her breath. Chloe was taking her tray to the table where Gemma and her friends were sitting!

"Now *that's* a nice coincidence," said Nibs, swishing her tail. But as soon as Chloe sat down, she pulled out her iPod and stuck in her earplugs. Maddy groaned. Her cousin really wasn't making this easy!

Then her ears pricked up as she heard what Gemma and her friends were saying.

"Oh, you and your stupid fantasy novels!" the blonde girl teased Gemma. "You should try reading a good romance instead of stuff about mouldy old dungeons all the time."

"They're not like that at all!" protested Gemma good-naturedly. She was flipping through a book with a dragon on the cover. "Honestly, Izzy, you should give fantasy a chance sometime – I bet you'd really like it."

Chloe's purple and silver handbag sat on the empty chair between her and Gemma. Maddy's eyes flew to it. She could just see the corner of Chloe's book sticking out! Leaning over, she eased it from the bag and tossed it onto the floor near Gemma's feet.

Bang! All the girls jumped at the noise. Chloe yanked her earplugs out, staring at the book in confusion. "Oh, sorry – it must have dropped out somehow."

But Gemma had already picked it up with a grin. "Hey, I love this author! Have you read any of her other stuff?"

Chloe looked startled as she took the book back. "Um – well, yes, loads of it, actually."

"Me too!" exclaimed Gemma. "Which is your favourite?"

"Gem! We were just going to the library, remember?" said the tall blonde girl as she and the other girl stood up. "Would you like to come?" she asked Chloe politely.

Maddy held her breath. Her cousin shoved the book back into her bag, her cheeks reddening. "Uh, no – that's OK," she mumbled.

Gemma looked disappointed. Reaching for her own bag, she pulled out a tiny notebook and wrote something down. "Listen, here's my mobile number," she said, handing a piece of paper to Chloe. "Why don't you text me sometime? We could

talk about other authors we like, or something."

Maddy punched the air invisibly as Gemma left with her friends. Hurrah! Gemma really seemed to want to be friends with Chloe. Their plan was going to work!

"Wait," whispered Nibs. "We're not there yet."

Maddy's smile died as she saw the disbelieving grimace on Chloe's face. "Yeah, right," her cousin muttered. "She'd probably laugh at me if I actually texted her."

Crumpling up the bit of paper, Chloe shoved it into her

empty sandwich packet. Maddy could have shrieked with frustration. When Chloe wasn't looking, she quickly rescued the mobile number – but her heart felt heavy.

Chloe seemed determined not to make any friends . . . and that meant that Maddy had no idea how to stop her from running away.

"Don't worry, we'll think of something else," said Nibs that evening.

Maddy sighed. She was sitting beside the doll's house, with Nibs perched on the tiny chimney as usual.

"*What*, though?" she said gloomily.

"Something will come up," promised the cat. "It always does." She cocked her tiny head to one side as she reflected. "Well . . . usually."

146

Maddy made a face. Though Mum
hadn't suspected anything when she'd
picked her up in front of the primary
school that afternoon, Maddy knew
that she daren't try such a trick again.
She'd been lucky to get away with
it once!

Chloe had barely spoken at all on
the way home. She'd just stared out of
the car window, listening to her iPod.

Remembering, Maddy felt an
anxious pang. She had the
uncomfortable feeling that her cousin
was just as keen to run away as
before. She hadn't helped her at all.

Maddy looked down. "I suppose
– I suppose you really wish that our
plan had worked," she said haltingly.
"I mean . . . I know you're in a hurry
to have the problem over with." She

didn't add, *Even though we've only barely got to know each other.*

Nibs gave Maddy a keen look, as if she had spoken the unsaid words after all. "Lift me up," she said.

Maddy did so, feeling Nibs's slight furry weight as the little cat stepped onto her palm. Slowly she raised her hand to her face.

"Now, then," said Nibs when she was at eye-level. "You must understand that the three of us are *always* anxious to solve whatever problem we're faced with. It's the only way we can reach our ultimate goal, which is very important to us."

"What goal?" whispered Maddy. Nibs's eyes staring into hers looked very serious.

Nibs shook her head. "I've said enough. But, Maddy, if you and I didn't have a task to complete, I'd be very happy to stay here with you. You're a nice girl – even if you do need to be kept away from handkerchiefs!" she added with a feline chuckle.

Maddy smiled. "Oh, Nibs, *may* I stroke you?" she burst out.

149

Chapter Seven

"Of course," purred Nibs, swishing her tail against Maddy's palm. "I'd be delighted!"

Chapter Eight

The rest of that week passed
without Maddy and Nibs coming
any closer to solving the problem.
Though terribly worried about her
cousin, Maddy enjoyed spending
time with Nibs. The little cat often
rode around the house on her
shoulder now, safely hidden by her
hair. And, as Maddy found out, she
loved to have her chin scratched! She
would close her eyes dreamily, her

purrs sounding like a pigeon cooing.

But all the time, Maddy was uncomfortably aware that Saturday was approaching. And if Nibs was right, that was when Chloe would try to run away.

"Mum, can I go shopping today?" Chloe asked on Saturday morning.

Maddy looked up from her breakfast sharply. Suddenly the toast she was chewing tasted like sawdust. The shopping centre was right beside the train station!

A surprised smile lit Aunt Lily's face. "Yes, I suppose so," she said. "Is there something special that you—"

"Can I go too?" blurted out Maddy.

Chloe's face darkened. "*No*," she said.

152

Aunt Lily shook her head. "Chloe, what's got into you lately? Of course Maddy can go if she wants to!"

Chloe slumped down in her seat, scowling. Reaching her hand into her pocket, Maddy touched Nibs's cool ceramic form. This was it, she was sure of it! No matter what happened today, she'd have to stick to her cousin like glue.

When Mum drove them to the shops
an hour later, Maddy wasn't surprised
to see that Chloe had her large purple
and silver bag with her – and that it
looked very fat, as if it were packed
full.

Maddy nibbled her thumb as she
stared anxiously at the bag. If only
she could knock it over somehow, so
that Mum and Aunt Lily could see
what was inside! But her cousin had it
on her lap, gripping it tightly.

"What do you want to buy, Chloe?"
asked Aunt Lily, turning round to look
at her.

Chloe jumped. "Oh! Nothing – I
just want to look around," she said.

To Maddy's amazement, once
they got to the shops Chloe seemed
friendlier than she had been all week.

"Can Maddy and I go off on our own together for a bit?" she asked. She shot Maddy a smile.

Maddy stared at her. Why was she acting so nice all of a sudden?

Mum hardly looked up from the rack of dresses that she and Aunt Lily were flipping through. "Yes, if you stay together. Why don't you meet us at McDonald's at one o'clock, and we'll all get some lunch?"

"OK . . ." Chloe hesitated, looking at her mother. "Um . . . bye, Mum," she said.

Aunt Lily glanced up in surprise. "Bye, honey. Have fun!"

Chloe nodded. For a moment Maddy thought her cousin looked uncertain, as if she might be changing her mind . . . and then she linked her arm through Maddy's. "Come on, cuz."

Once they were out of sight of their mothers, Chloe dropped her arm. "Why don't you go to the toy store or something?" she said flatly. "I want to be on my own for a bit."

Maddy swallowed. "But—"

Before she could get any further, Chloe had gone striding off. Maddy raced to catch up with her. "Wait!" she gasped, skipping round in front of her cousin. "Mum said to stick together, remember?"

Chloe's blonde eyebrows drew together in a scowl. "So?" she said, trying to dodge round Maddy.

Maddy stood her ground. "So – so I think that's what we should do," she said desperately. "Can't I go with you?"

Chloe pushed her firmly to one side. "Maddy, I'm serious – I want to be alone for a while! Now, *don't* follow me, or you'll be sorry. Understand?"

Maddy watched in alarm as Chloe hurried off. Quickly she ducked into a bookshop and crouched behind a tall display of bestsellers. *Shadow magic, conceal me!* she thought feverishly, touching the ceramic cat in her pocket.

The tingling feeling flowed through her. Alive again, Nibs bounded invisibly up to her shoulder. "Hurry!" she yowled in Maddy's ear. "We have to catch her!"

Maddy ran after Chloe, darting in and out of crowds of unsuspecting shoppers. Nibs clung to her jumper, neatly balancing herself with her tail. "Oh! Did you feel that breeze?" Maddy heard one woman exclaim.

Suddenly she skidded to a stop as she spotted Chloe. She was standing in front of a large map of the shopping centre, studying it intently. A moment later she set off again, this time with Maddy close behind.

She walked straight to the train station.

Though Maddy had expected it, her heart twisted anxiously. She followed

Shadow Magic

Chloe up the concrete steps from the street. Once inside the station, her cousin faltered. With a nervous glance at the ticket counter, she headed instead for the automatic machines.

Maddy hovered invisibly next to Chloe as she started pressing buttons. DESTINATION? asked the screen.

There was a keyboard on the machine. Chloe started to type. Leaning over quickly, Maddy began jabbing keys at random. LOLLOPLOPLOP appeared on the screen.

NO SUCH DESTINATION FOUND, flashed the machine.

Chloe's jaw dropped. "*Huh?*" She tried again.

MOOOOOOOOO, typed Maddy.

Chloe swallowed, and backed away a step. "O-kay . . ." she muttered. "Maybe – maybe I'll try a different machine."

At the next machine she stood close to the keyboard, guarding it as she typed. Standing helplessly to one side,

160

Maddy gritted her teeth in frustration – and then her cousin took several notes out of her wallet. *Of course!*

Gazing down at the machine, Chloe started to feed in the notes, one by one. As she did so, Maddy carefully eased a ten-pound note out of Chloe's hand, quickly slipping it into her own pocket.

"Excellent!" whispered Nibs warmly.

AMOUNT REMAINING: £10, flashed the screen.

"What?" Chloe peered into her wallet again. "But – I know I had the right amount!" she gasped. She stared wildly at the floor around her, dropping to her knees and searching all around the machine.

"Have you lost something?" asked a woman at the next machine.

"Ten pounds!" burst out Chloe. She looked close to tears. "It was part of my birthday money, and I need the rest of it to catch a bus!"

The woman frowned doubtfully. "Are you travelling alone, dear?" she asked.

Chloe's cheeks turned bright red. She scrambled to her feet. "Uh – no," she muttered, hitting CANCEL on the machine. "I'm just . . . buying it for my mother." Taking her remaining notes out of the machine again, she hastily left the station.

Hurrah! thought Maddy, hurrying after Chloe as she jogged down the station steps. They had done it . . . at least, for now. But they still needed to make Chloe happy about staying, somehow, or else she'd just try again.

Maddy looked down at the little cat on her shoulder. "Nibs, how long do you think we have before—"

"Watch out!" hissed Nibs.

"Oof!" exclaimed Maddy as she crashed full-speed into Chloe's back. The invisibility left her. Chloe spun round with a shriek – and then anger came over her face like a thunder-cloud.

"You've been following me!" she shouted.

"No, I haven't," mumbled Maddy. She could feel the ceramic Nibs about to topple off her shoulder, and she hastily caught the little cat.

"You *have*," insisted Chloe. She shook Maddy's arm. "What did you see? Tell me! *Now!*"

"All right!" Maddy burst out. "I – I saw you go into the train station and try to buy a ticket. Oh, Chloe, you *can't* run away – it's really dangerous! Please, please, promise me you won't!" Her throat felt tight with tears.

Chloe was staring at her. "It wasn't you who . . ." she started, and then

shook her head. "No, it couldn't have been! Now listen, Maddy. If you tell *anyone* about this, I will *never, ever* speak to you again. Got it?"

She looked so furious that Maddy felt frightened. She nodded mutely.

"Good," snapped Chloe. She turned and stalked away.

Maddy struggled to keep up with her. "But – but, Chloe, you haven't said that you won't—"

"Drop it!" snarled Chloe.

Maddy fell silent, disheartened. Clearly she hadn't changed her cousin's mind at all. Chloe was still determined to run away.

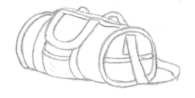

Chapter Nine

That afternoon Maddy curled up on the sofa with a book, trying to keep an eye on Chloe without her cousin noticing. Though Chloe had put on a bright face once they were back with their mothers, she hadn't said a single word to Maddy since the scene at the train station.

Maddy stared down at the pages, pretending to read. She looked up quickly as her cousin came into the lounge. Dad, Jack and Uncle Greg were in there as well, watching a football match on TV.

"Dad?" said Chloe, standing in front of Uncle Greg.

"Hmm?" He craned his head round her, trying to see the screen.

"Dad, there was this top that I really liked at the shops," said Chloe, shifting from foot to foot. "Only . . . it was ten pounds more than I had. Do you think I could borrow the money?"

No! Maddy wanted to shout. She sat there frozen, unable to say a word. On the TV one of the teams scored a goal, and Dad, Uncle Greg and Jack cheered.

"*Dad,*" urged Chloe. "Can I? It's important. I mean, I really want to buy it."

168

"What's that? Ten pounds?"
Without taking his eyes off the screen,
Uncle Greg reached for his wallet and
fished out a ten-pound note. "There
you go, love."

Chloe's face shone with relief.
"Thanks, Dad!" Her eyes met

Maddy's, and she gave her a hard look. Maddy went cold. She knew the look meant, *Don't you dare tell, or else!*

Chloe went back into the study. Maddy stared after her, her thoughts spinning. Would her cousin still try to run away today? They didn't live *that* far from the train station – her cousin could easily walk it if she wanted to.

What was she going to do? She couldn't just let Chloe leave, but if she said anything, her cousin would never speak to her again! Even if they weren't really friends any more, the thought was still very painful.

Maddy felt a warm wriggle as Nibs came to life in her pocket. With everyone's eyes glued to the TV, she sneakily placed the tiny cat on her shoulder, pulling her long hair in front to hide her.

Nibs tickled her whiskers against Maddy's ear, comforting her. "It's not over yet, you know," she whispered. "Last-minute successes are my speciality!"

Maddy suppressed a grin. At least she was friends with Nibs now. That was something, at least. Suddenly she went very still. What was it Nibs had said? *Sometimes one friend is all you need.*

Gemma! The thought sizzled through Maddy like lightning. Perhaps Chloe wasn't going to text Gemma – but Maddy could, if only it wasn't too late! Scrambling off the sofa, she pounded up the stairs to her room.

"What is it?" demanded Nibs, clinging tightly to her shoulder.

Maddy quickly explained her idea as she rummaged through her school bag. Nibs's green eyes gleamed. She hopped over and peered into the bag, swishing her tail for balance. "Now, that's the sort of thinking I like!"

Oh, *where* was it? Maddy was sure she'd put the little piece of paper in her bag . . . *there*! Maddy grabbed it in relief. "Come on," she said to Nibs. "We've no time to lose!"

Going shadowy almost felt like second nature now. Ghost-like, Maddy slipped down the stairs again – though her

father, brother and uncle were all
making so much noise that she wasn't
sure why she worried about keeping
quiet!

Luckily the study door was open.
As Maddy peeped inside, her heart
seemed to leap
into her throat.
Chloe was
gone! Then she
saw the purple
and silver bag
on the desk,
and relaxed. Her cousin must have
just gone to the loo.

Spotting a mobile lying beside the
bag, Maddy hurried over and flipped
it open. "Better hide, in case she
comes back," advised Nibs. "*You're
invisible – but the phone isn't.*"

Chapter Nine

"Oh, right," whispered Maddy. She darted behind the sofa – and then on impulse took Chloe's bag with her as well, shoving it out of sight behind the curtains.

HI, she typed into Chloe's phone. I'M CHLOE, THE NEW GIRL WHO LIKES READING FANTASY TOO! WHY DON'T U COME ROUND THIS AFTERNOON? I'M STAYING AT 12 WILLOW STREET, JUST ACROSS THE MEADOW FROM U!

Just as Maddy hit SEND, she heard Chloe come back into the study. "Hey, where's my bag?" said her cousin.

Hiding the phone underneath the sofa, Maddy quietly stood up and saw Chloe looking around in confusion.

"Jack, did you take my bag?" she asked loudly.

"Why would I want your stupid bag?" he called back from the lounge.

"I bet Maddy did it, then," exclaimed Chloe grimly, clenching her fists. Suddenly Maddy was extremely glad that she was invisible!

"No, she went upstairs a while ago," said Uncle Greg's voice. "You've probably just misplaced it— *Yes*!" He broke off as the TV commentator went wild.

Chloe spent ages searching for

175

the bag, grumbling to herself as she looked under the desk and in the cupboard. Finally she flipped the curtains aside, and let out a cry of relief. "*There* it is! Jack, you *did* hide it here, didn't you?"

"NO!" bellowed Jack from the next room.

Near Maddy's foot, the mobile beeped loudly as a text arrived. Chloe looked at the desk, and her face went slack with astonishment. "Huh? I'm sure I left it right there . . ."

As she went over to the desk, Maddy squatted down and flipped open the phone. A message from Gemma!

OK, I'LL ASK MY MUM. SEE U SOON MAYBE!

Maddy bit her lip. Oh, why couldn't Gemma have said for sure?

Chloe was searching on the desk, shoving things aside. "Now my *phone's* missing," she shouted. "Seriously, Jack, if you or Maddy are doing this, I *don't* think it's funny!"

"Be quiet, we're watching the game!" replied Jack.

Deleting both texts, Maddy hid the phone again. The longer Chloe was delayed looking for it, the better!

But this time she found it quickly,

pulling it out from under the sofa in just a few minutes. She stared at the screen in confusion, obviously wondering where the new text was.

Finally she shrugged. "Never mind," she muttered under her breath. "I'll text Chrissy once I'm on my way." She headed for the desk again, with Maddy following anxiously. What *now*?

"Her shoelaces!" hissed Nibs.

Of course! As Chloe paused to put her phone in her bag, Maddy quickly ducked down and knotted her laces together.

"Dad, can I go for a— *Oh!*" Chloe

cried out as she tripped over her
own feet. She went sprawling to the
floor.

"Are you OK?" called Uncle Greg.

Chloe had gone very pale, gawping
at her tied-together shoes. "I – I
don't understand," she whispered.

She shook her head hard. "I'm
going mad!" Hurriedly she tied her

laces correctly and then jumped up, grabbing her bag.

"I'm fine, Dad!" she said. She went to the study doorway, looking flustered. "Um – can I go for a walk?"

Uncle Greg nodded, his attention back on the game. "Yes, OK. Don't be long."

"I won't!" Holding her bag to her chest, Chloe hurried through the lounge.

No! Invisibly, Maddy raced after her. Without thinking, she launched herself at her cousin like a rugby player, tackling her to the ground just as she reached the front hallway.

"*Argh!*" screamed Chloe. Her bag went tumbling across the carpet.

Jumping up, Maddy grabbed it and shook it upside-down. Chloe's eyes bulged as her bag floated in the air, spilling clothes and books. "No, I've got to be dreaming this!" she gasped.

"Chloe, was that you?" called Aunt Lily's voice.

Just as Maddy dropped the bag, her aunt came rushing in from the kitchen, with Mum just behind her. At the same moment Dad and Uncle Greg appeared in the other doorway.

There was a stunned pause as the four adults stared down at the pile of clothes on the floor. Nibs had leaped clear as Maddy lunged, and now the tiny cat invisibly twitched a bus timetable into view.

Scooping Nibs up in her hand, Maddy slipped halfway up the stairs and became visible again, as though she were just coming down from her room. No one noticed her; all eyes were on her cousin.

Uncle Greg helped Chloe up. His

face was more serious than Maddy
had ever seen it. "Where were
you going?"

Chloe shrugged. "Nowhere," she
muttered.

Aunt Lily spotted the bus timetable
and gasped. "Chloe! You – you were
running away, weren't you?"

Chloe's face turned bright red.
For a moment Maddy thought her

cousin wouldn't answer. "Yes!" she exploded suddenly. "Yes, because I *hate* moving all the time! I never get to make any friends, never, and then I finally had one and we had to move!" Kicking her bag, she burst into tears.

Aunt Lily put her arms around her, looking shaken. "Oh, Chloe . . . I knew you were unhappy, but I had no idea it was *this* bad. You should have told us!"

"I tried!" sobbed Chloe. "But you and Dad just kept saying I'd get used to it. So I was going to go home, and Chrissy was going to hide me – we had it all planned out!"

Uncle Greg looked torn between anger and sympathy. "Chloe, you daft girl," he said, stroking her hair. "Don't you realize how dangerous that would have been?"

Chloe lifted her head from Aunt Lily's shoulder. "I don't care," she sniffed. "Dad, you don't know what it's like – it's *so* hard for me to make friends—"

"No, it's not! What about Gemma?" Maddy burst out.

Every head in the room turned to look at her. "Gemma?" echoed Chloe, her eyes wide. "How do *you* know

185

about Gemma?"

Maddy winced, realizing her mistake. "Um . . . I don't know. Didn't you mention her the other day?"

Chloe shook her head, looking baffled. "Why would I? I hardly even know her."

Just then there was a knock at the back door. "Who could *that* be?" muttered Dad, disappearing towards the kitchen. Maddy held her breath in hope.

Aunt Lily sighed as she wiped her daughter's tears away. "Sweetie, I know it can be hard to make friends sometimes, but no matter how unhappy you are, you *always* have to come to us."

Uncle Greg nodded. "This is very

serious, Chloe," he told her. "Running away is—"

He broke off as Dad reappeared, followed by a girl with a chestnut-brown ponytail. "Well . . . speak of the devil," he said with a confused glance at Maddy. "This is Gemma. She says Chloe invited her over."

"Hi, Chloe," said Gemma. Her brown eyes were bright and friendly.

"Thanks for your text. Mum said I could come over until dinner time."

There was a startled pause. Chloe's jaw dropped. Before she could say anything, Maddy caught her eye, nodding her head wildly.

Chloe slowly closed her mouth again. "Um – yeah," she said. "That's great. If . . . if that's OK?" She looked at her parents.

Aunt Lily and Uncle Greg exchanged a glance. Finally Uncle Greg nodded. "All right. But, Chloe, we're going to have to have a very serious talk later."

"I know," said Chloe, her cheeks reddening. Squatting down, she quickly scooped her things back into her bag, and then stood up, facing Gemma. "Um, would you like

188

to . . . watch a DVD on the computer or
something?"

Gemma nodded. "Or else we
could just talk," she added cheerfully
as they headed towards the study.
"You could tell me about your old
school."

"Which one?" asked Chloe with a
sudden giggle. All at once she darted

back into the hallway again, and gave both her parents a fierce hug. "I'm sorry," she said. "Really. I won't do it again."

Aunt Lily blinked as the two girls disappeared into the study. "You know . . . I'm not actually sure what's just happened here," she said.

"Join the club," said Mum, rubbing her temples. She gazed at Maddy, started to say something, and then shook her head instead.

Maddy shrugged, and tried to smile. "Just a lucky guess," she said.

When Maddy went upstairs after dinner that night, Nibs wasn't in the Barbie house. After a quick search, Maddy spotted the open window and smiled despite herself. Settling down

190

on her bed, she picked up her book
and started to read.

There was a knock on the door, and
Chloe poked her head in. "Hi," she
said. "Can I come in?"

Maddy looked up in surprise.
"Sure."

Chloe sat down next to her, tracing
a pattern on the duvet. "This is,
um . . . a pretty colour," she said
finally.

Maddy couldn't resist asking,

"Aren't you too grown up for pink now?"

Chloe cringed. "Oh, Maddy, I'm really sorry!" she exclaimed. "I've been acting like such a jerk. I was just so homesick! I thought I was going to burst into tears all the time, and the only way I could stop it was to act like I didn't care about anything."

Relief rushed through Maddy like a sparkling brook. "You mean . . . you don't think you're too grown up to be friends with me now?" she asked shyly.

Chloe shook her head so hard that her blonde hair flew about her face. "No way! Maddy, I didn't want to share your room with you because I was afraid you'd find out what I was planning, that's all. Plus . . . plus I

Jopping down from her bed,
lled the brightly coloured sign
om underneath and presented
er cousin with a flourish.
."

oe smiled as she gazed down at
owers and rainbows. "Thanks,

cuz," she
murmured.
"It's
beautiful!"
She glanced
at Maddy.
"Do you

ık . . . I mean, would you still
e me to share your room with you
ile we're here? 'Cause I'd really,
lly like to!"

Yes!" cried Maddy, bouncing on
r toes.

was still crying myself to sleep every
night." She looked down.

Oh, poor Chloe! Maddy squeezed
her cousin's arm tightly. "It must be
really hard, moving around so much,"
she said. "I'd hate it too."

Chloe cleared her throat. "But,
Maddy, guess what? Dad says that
he's going to talk to them at work
about making this job a permanent
one. So who knows – maybe I'll get
to stay here for a while."

"Chloe! That's brilliant!" Maddy
bounced excitedly up onto her knees.

Her cousin's
eyes were
shining.
"Yeah,
it's not
bad, is it?

Especially now that I'm friends with Gemma. She's really great, Maddy – we talked for hours! She wants me to sit with her and her friends on Monday. She thinks we'll all get on really well."

Maddy's own smile felt like it was stretching right across her face. "So . . . you don't want to run away any more?"

Chloe gave an embarrassed grimace. "No . . . I guess it was a pretty stupid idea! I've promised Mum and Dad that I'll never even think of it again." She sighed. "I'll still really miss Chrissy, but Mum says I can visit her over the holidays."

Maddy nodded sympathetically. She knew how much she'd miss Rachel if she ever had to leave her, even if

she was luck friends.

There was a gave her a side Maddy," she sa stupid question weird things ha lately, and . . . w anything to do w

Maddy widene to look at the pink Nibs's bed in it. " asked.

Chloe's sceptical with confusion. "I g imagining things," s She stood up to leave almost forgot! Do you welcome sign you ma

A huge grin burst ac

face. H she pu out fr it to h "Here Ch the fl

thi lik wh re

he

"Great!" said Chloe happily. "I'll tell Aunt Jenny tomorrow. I can hardly wait!"

Maddy felt like singing as Chloe headed back downstairs. She and Nibs had done it; they'd really done it. They had helped her cousin – and, even better, now she and Chloe were friends again!

Then Maddy's smile faded as she realized something. The problem had been solved . . . and that meant it was time for Nibs to leave.

About half an hour later, Nibs appeared on the windowsill with a faint *thump*. "Isn't it a lovely night?" she said. She strolled along the wooden pathway like a tiny panther. "I just went for one last prowl."

Maddy jumped out of bed. "I guessed you had," she said, going over to the window.

She put her hand out and Nibs stepped onto it, purring. Her glossy black fur felt cool from the night air as Maddy stroked it with a finger. She sat cuddling the little cat for some time, scratching her under the chin the way Nibs loved.

Finally Nibs sighed. "It's time, Maddy."

Maddy's throat felt tight. "Oh, Nibs," she said, cupping the little cat against her cheek. "I don't want to say goodbye just yet!"

Nibs's forest-green eyes gleamed up at her. "Nor me. But soon it will be my turn again." She gave a feline chuckle. "This was a first for me, you know – being trapped in a handkerchief before even saying hello! But you've done well, Maddy. Thank you."

Maddy couldn't help it; she wiped a tear away. Why on earth had she wanted Nibs to be like Greykin at first? She already had a Greykin. But Nibs – the midnight-black huntress with

the dry sense of humour, so aloof until
you got to know her, and so lovely
once you did – was one of a kind, and
Maddy knew she was going to miss
her terribly.

"Goodbye for now, dear one," said
Nibs. Stretching up on Maddy's palm,
she touched her tiny nose to Maddy's,
soft as a butterfly's kiss. "Don't be
sad."

"Goodbye, Nibs," whispered
Maddy. Giving the sleek black fur

one last stroke, she took the little cat
over to the desk and set her down
gently.

Nibs sauntered over to the other two
cats, waving her slim tail. Settling
down beside Greykin and the tabby,
she arranged herself so that her paws
and tail were entwined with theirs.

"Bye," mouthed Maddy, wiggling
her fingers in a sad wave.

Nibs's fur shimmered as she slowly
became ceramic once more. Just
before she did, she winked at Maddy
– and then she was gone, smooth and
stiff once more.

Maddy swallowed hard. It was
wonderful having the cats, but it hurt
so much when they had to leave! Still,
even with the pain of parting, she
knew she'd never choose not to have

them. Maybe the cost of magic was a little sadness now and then.

Maddy's gaze fell on the last of the trio: the long-haired tabby with white chest and paws. She picked him up, looking into his bright golden eyes. Though only painted, they seemed to sparkle.

"I'm really looking forward to meeting you," Maddy told him. And next time, she decided, she wouldn't expect this cat to be like either Greykin *or* Nibs – instead she'd wait and see what he was like, and get to know him for himself!

"I hope it's soon." Maddy smiled as she touched the cat's smooth white nose. "Because I can hardly wait!"

THE END

Don't miss
Pocket Cats: *Paw Power*

When Maddy buys three tiny ceramic cats at an antique market, she knows they're special. But it's not until she gets them home that she realizes just how special they are—when one of them *comes to life!* Greykin explains that the Pocket Cats are there to help Maddy, and she and Greykin have a tricky problem to solve: there's a new girl in school who's being picked on by the class bully. Will a little bit of magic and a lot of courage be enough to stop the scariest girl in school?

Don't miss
Pocket Cats: *Feline Charm*

Ollie's tingling whiskers tell him that Maddy's best friend is about to give up on ballet, even though she loves it. So Maddy uses her new magic power to boost Rachel's confidence. But when Rachel lands the star part in the ballet school's big show, Maddy is desperately jealous.

On opening night, when Rachel needs the cat magic more than ever, will Maddy be strong enough to put her best friend first?